This book belongs to:

_____

For Primrose, the famous artist

Digital art by Callaway Animation Studios under the direction of David Kirk in collaboration with Nelvana Limited.

This book is based on the TV episode "Wiggle's Squiggles," written by Steve Sullivan, from the animated TV series *Miss Spider's Sunny Patch Friends* on Nick Jr., a Nelvana Limited/Absolute Pictures Limited co-production in association with Callaway Arts & Entertainment, based on the Miss Spider books by David Kirk.

Nicholas Callaway, President and Publisher
Cathy Ferrara, Managing Editor and Production Director
Toshiya Masuda, Art Director • Nelson Gomez, Director of Digital Services
Joya Rajadhyaksha, Associate Editor • Amy Cloud, Associate Editor
Cara Paul, Digital Artist • Aharon Charnov, Digital Artist • Bill Burg, Digital Artist
Alex Ballas, Assistant Designer • Raphael Shea, Art Assistant • Krupa Jhaveri, Design Assistant • Masako Ebata, Designer

Special thanks to the Nelvana staff, including Doug Murphy, Scott Dyer, Tracy Ewing, Pam Lehn, Tonya Lindo, Mark Picard, Susie Grondin, Luis Lopez, Eric Pentz, and Georgina Robinson.

Library of Congress Cataloging-in-Publication Data available upon request.

Distributed in the United States by Viking Children's Books.

Callaway Arts & Entertainment, its Callaway logotype, and Callaway & Kirk Company LLC are trademarks.

ISBN 0-448-44519-0

Visit Callaway Arts & Entertainment at www.callaway.com

10 9 8 7 6 5 4 3 2 1   06 07 08 09 10

Printed in China

Miss Spider's

Wiggle's Squiggles

David Kirk

CALLAWAY

NEW YORK

2006

One sunshiny day in Sunny Patch, Miss Spider's little bugs were busy gathering brightly colored flowers and berries to squish into paint.

"I can't wait for our first art class tomorrow!" Wiggle exclaimed as he picked a daisy. "I think I might be a really good artist!"

"Just keep those daisies away from me!" Holley sniffled. "They make me sneeze— AAHHHH CHOOO!"

As art class began, Professor Mantis told everybuggy about the big art show he planned for their work. There would even be a special ribbon for the best picture!

"But . . . but . . . how do you start to paint?" Wiggle stammered.

"It's simple!" replied Mr. Mantis. "Find something you like and then let your imagination take over!"

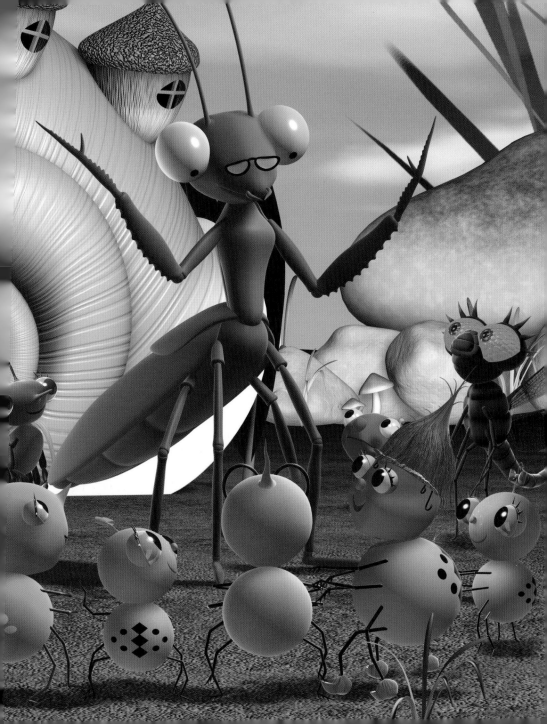

"**J**ust look at the daisy," Mr. Mantis suggested, "and paint how you feel."

Wiggle dipped his brush into some bright yellow paint, then splattered a blob on his canvas.

"That's it!" he exclaimed. "I'm an artist!"

Wiggle stood next to his finished painting, smiling to himself. My painting looks just how I feel, he thought. Sunny!

That's when he saw Shimmer's picture.

"Wow," he said. "That looks just like a real daisy."

"Thanks, Wiggle. Can I see yours?" she asked.

Suddenly, Wiggle felt ashamed of his squiggly painting. It didn't look anything like Shimmer's. It didn't look like anything at all!

"Um, well, maybe not," he spluttered. "I'm not exactly sure it's done yet."

That night, Wiggle lay awake worrying about his painting.

"Hey, Shimmer," he whispered.
"Can you . . . paint my picture for me?"

"But, Wiggle! Then it wouldn't be your picture!"

"But I just can't paint," Wiggle said sadly.

"Everybuggy can paint!"
Shimmer yawned.

"Everybuggy except me," Wiggle sighed.

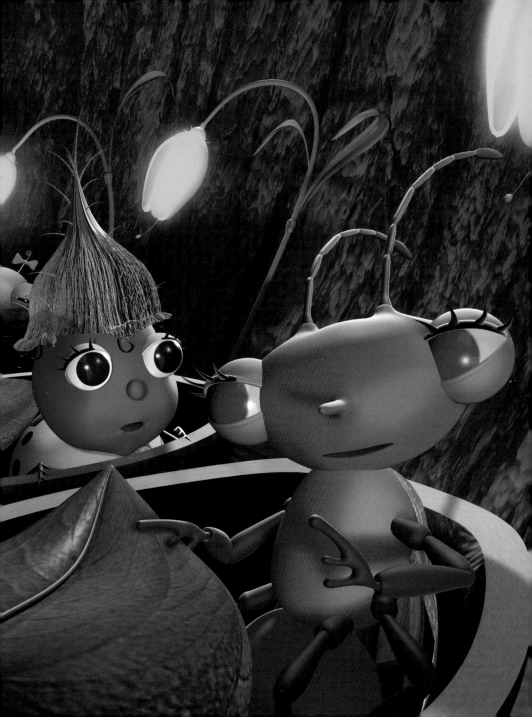

The next morning, no matter how hard he tried, Wiggle couldn't make his painting look like Shimmer's.

Then he had an idea. Maybe he didn't need to paint the daisy. He dragged the daisy over to his easel and glued it onto a new bark canvas.

"Now *that* looks like a daisy!" he exclaimed proudly. "Because it is a daisy!"

"**L**ook at my painting, everybuggy!" Wiggle called when he got home.

Wow!" everyone gasped.

My, my," Holley said, scooting in for a closer look. "What an excellent artist you are, Wi-wi-wi . . . ah, ah, AH CHOO!"

Holley's sneeze sent Wiggle's painting flying into the air. The daisy petals rained down on everybuggy.

I-I guess I didn't exactly paint it," Wiggle sniffled as he shuffled off.

"Wiggle, why didn't you try to paint
the flower?" Miss Spider asked.

"I did try, Mom," Wiggle said, showing her his
squiggly painting. "But it's no good. Look!"

"Oh my goodness, Wiggle," she smiled.
"This is a beautiful painting!"

"But it doesn't look like a
daisy at all," Wiggle sighed.

"A painting doesn't have to look exactly like
something to be beautiful," Miss Spider
explained. "Your painting is good because
it's more than just a picture of a daisy; it's
a picture of how you see it!"

ater on, the art show was already nderway when Miss Spider and Wiggle rived.

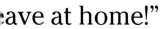wish my painting could be here," Wiggle iid sadly.

)o you have room for one more?" Holley ;ked Mr. Mantis, holding up Wiggle's ainting. "I thought it was too good to :ave at home!"

"We always have room for a painting that's so colorful and delightfully different!" Mr. Mantis exclaimed.

"But . . . can you tell it's a daisy?" Wiggle asked.

"It's not just a daisy, Wiggle," Mr. Mantis explained. "It's your daisy. And I think it needs just one more thing . . ."

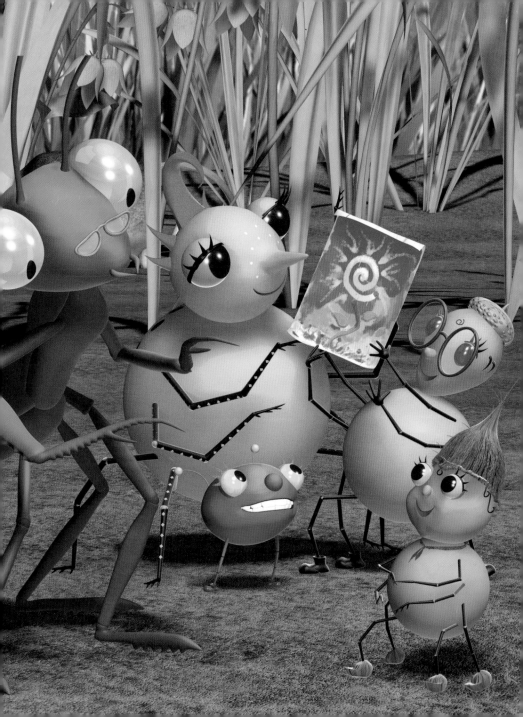

"A blue ribbon!" Mr. Mantis exclaimed. "For being the most original."

"Wow!" Wiggle said excitedly. "I'm a real artist!"

"Yay, Wiggle!" everyone cheered. "Great job!"

"Look, Mom!" Wiggle said. "Nobuggy painted their daisy the same way. And I like them all!"

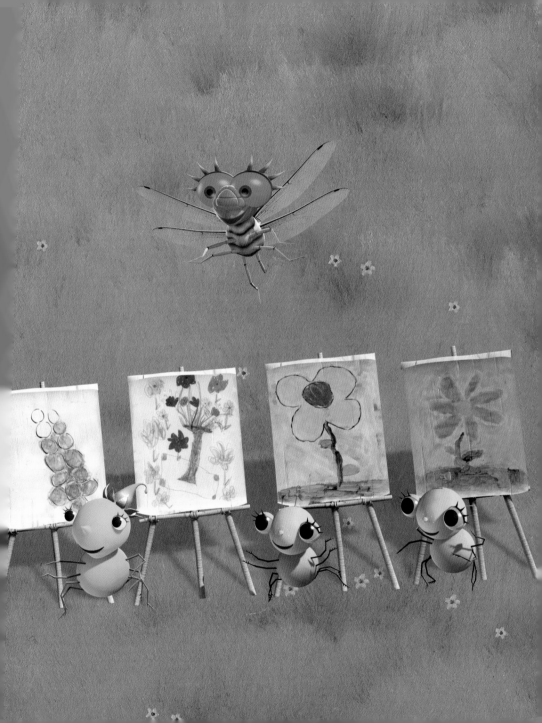

Miss Spider agreed. "Everybuggy sees things differently, Wiggle. That's what makes art so much fun!"

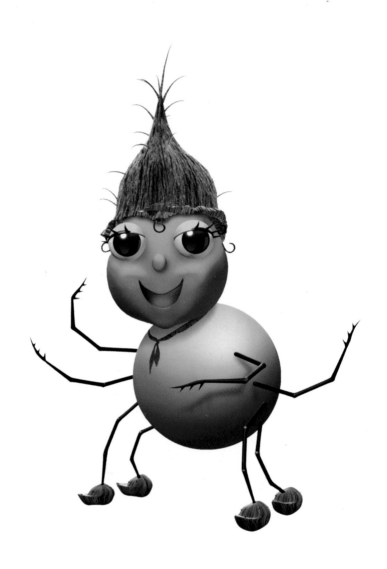

THE END